FORGIVE ME
FORGIVE ME NOT

VOLUME 2

BY: PAMELA TUCKER

Forgive Me Forgive Me Not Volume 2

Copyright © 2019 by Pamela Tucker

"Scripture references are taken from the New International Version, unless otherwise stated".

Printed in the United States of America.

First printing, 2019

ISBN 978-0-578-508146

ReStart Enterprise
restartenterprise2017@gmail.com

ACKNOWLEDGEMENTS

———————— ❧❧❧❧ ————————

First, I thank God for his grace, mercy, and strength to complete these chapters of my life, without him, none of this would have been possible.

I thank him for the beautiful family he's blessed me with, 3 beautiful daughters Olivia, Antiea, Breanna, and my precious granddaughter Peyton. My siblings Mary, Jimmy and Brenda.

Thank you all for your encouragement, support, push and your prayers. I Love you All.

To my Leaders Apostle Travis & Pastor Stephanie Jennings, I thank you both for your prayers and prophetic words that keep me moving towards the Life God has for me. I Love you both.

I would like to express my deepest appreciation to the following people who worked with me to make this book a reality.

Rachelle Cherry, Thank you for taking the time out to discuss my book with me, also for proofreading " and editing your support, encouragement, and prayers.

Trena L. Baker, Thank you for reading, the words on the pages of my book numerous times until it was finished, and for your support and your prayers.

Prophetess Carrie M.Dumas, Thank you for asking me what's going on with the book so many times, That meant a lot,it pushed me to continue to write. Thank you for believing, encouraging and praying for me.

To family and friends who encouraged me in any way . Thank you

I would also like to extend my deepest gratitude to the following businesses.

Great Escapes by Shay, Thank you for reading my book and your feedback, support and setting me up some R&R time that was much needed.

Phenomenal Life, Thank you for listening, reading, proofreading, editing, your encouragements, and prayers.

NeverMind Creating Productions, Thank you for making an extraordinary youtube trailer of this book. I am excited about the next project.

Cover Art Designer, Calvin Finklea Creative Photography & Graphics

I truly appreciate you for seeing a part of my life journey in a picture and creating such an absolutely beautiful representation of it. Thank you.

HOW DID I GET HERE

———— ❧✦❧ ————

I was here at the home going service of my first born Carla. Everyone that loved her was there regardless of their thoughts about me. These thoughts were vocalized, however, the second the service was over some said "Arianna, you should have made another decision," some said I didn't love my baby Others said that I had killed my baby.

I could not understand how they could be so cruel. How could they not see what their words were doing to me. How could they not comprehend the depth of pain and grief, I was experiencing, Didn't they realize that I was a mother burying her child. The words they spoke against me out of their pain and anger were attacking my heart.

I lived in a state of grief and the pain of it was unbearable. In my mind, all I heard was, "It's all your fault, AJ. You killed your baby. You killed your first born." These endless thoughts tormented me. I took pills to sleep. I took pills to stay alert.

I had to fight through the fog of pain and grief and get to my secret place to cry out.

In this cry, I learned I had to FORGIVE.

I CAN'T BREATHE! "GOD HELP ME!

CHAPTER ONE:

————— ❦ —————

THE DECISION I MADE

Middle school was long behind me. My now 14-year-old mind was flooded with queries of why life had been so heartbreaking to me. I moved on from it and went about my days as if nothing annoyed me. I was also bothered by my dad continually referring to me as strange.

High school only added to my troubles. I wanted to wear pants as the other girls did. I didn't want to look like anyone else, but I did want to wear different things besides dresses and skirts. My mom would tell me that my butt was too big to wear pants. I didn't care; when I wanted to wear pants, I borrowed a pair of jeans from my best friend, Sabrina, and changed at her house, which was around the corner from my house.

I'm tired of sneaking around. I desperately wanted my own pants. I spent the weekend of spring break pleading with my mom to get me some pants.

"Arianna, we don't have money to waste on pants for you."

My cousin, Danielle was over at the house. Danielle was fashionable. She was grown, in her twenties, Danielle was in the living room talking to my dad, her uncle as I continued pleading my case to my mom.

My mom did not change her mind about giving me the money to get the pants, so I gave up. I left the kitchen and headed out to the porch.

"Now you know your mom doesn't wantchu' wearing no pants, showing off all your goods AJ."

Danielle was standing on the threshold of the front door, looking down at me as I sat on the porch. She had rested her 5'5 frame against the door panel and begin talking to me as she applied her lip gloss. Her remarks made it even more evident that she had heard the conversation I was having with my mom.

"If you want some pants, I'll get em' for you AJ."

She had finished applying her gloss and was sitting on the stoop next to me. Her words were music to my ears but how was she going to do that when she was here borrowing money from my dad. I really wanted some pants. Danielle was offering, and I never took anything from her before, so I didn't see the problem. She was my cousin, so I didn't see the harm. I didn't know where she was going to get the money, but I really wanted my on pants.

We sat there and hashed out a plan of how and when she would come to get me to go to the mall.

She said that Friday morning would be the only time she was available to take me.

I was excited! I jumped from my seated position, ready to tell my mom, but Danielle stopped me immediately. "You can't tell your folks AJ. They'll be mad at me, for taking you out of school." And I just 'borrowed money from your dad.

I was apprehensive and she could tell. She took my hand and pulled me back down to sit next to her.

'"There's no need to tell em.' You'll be back before they even know that you're gone, and you will have brand new clothes to flaunt."

I thought about it for a minute and agreed shortly thereafter. I thought to myself Danielle was an answer to my prayers. I could see it, no more dresses, all pants. As crazy as it sounds, I could not wait for school to start back. I was ready for Friday morning to come so I could get my pants.

***

Quicker than expected, Friday had come. I jumped out of bed ready to get my day started. I was about to get me some new clothes. As usual, I got myself dressed and ready for school. I comb my hair and ate breakfast like it was any other day. Once my morning prep routine was over, I gathered my books, and got my backpack, and made my way down to the bus stop— only this time, I wasn't really going to the bus stop.

That day when Danielle told me she would take me to the mall, we came up with a plan of where she would get me and at what time. We decided that I would go to LaTonya's house. She was a friend of mine in the neighborhood. Her house was right by the bus stop, so walking in that direction was normal. The plan was for me to stay with them and wait for Danielle to come to get me.

I stuck with the plan, and it went off without a hitch. After a few minutes of waiting with LaTonya and her sisters, Danielle had pulled up. She did not wait for me long. I was already headed outside because LaTonya's dad was home and he gave me the creeps. He always referred to the way my dresses fit me or how I was shaped. He was a perv of a man.

I jumped in the car, and we sped off down the street. We got to the stoplight of Rex and Stagecoach road when Danielle told me that she had to make a stop before the mall. She said she needed to go to West Side that was one heck of a drive coming from South Georgia on a school day.

The traffic was guaranteed to be horrible. The drive didn't faze me; I just wanted to get to a mall already. I was hoping that this stop did not take long.

The ride was over an hour and thirty minutes. We pulled up to a gray duplex, with a blue door.

Danielle told me to come inside because it was too hot to sit in the car. It wasn't scolding hot, but because I didn't know how long she was going to be, I decided to get out and follow her inside.

"This is my grandma Pam's house. We're not gonna be here long. I need to handle something right quick."

Danielle and I didn't hang out much. Matter of fact, we didn't hang out at all outside of when she came over to our house to see my dad every blue moon. None of my siblings had ever seen her side of the family. We only heard mentions of them from the stories my dad told. To be in her grandmother's house was surreal to me. As I entered the room, the linoleum floor made the grossest sound as I walked across it to follow Danielle

It was as if something sticky had spilled and not cleaned well.

Danielle left me in the living room and headed to the back of the house. I sat there waiting, hoping that whatever she was doing, that she was doing it quickly. Within minutes she had appeared in the room she had left me in.

"AJ I've got to handle something really quick. I need you to stay here. I'll be right back." Danielle said hastily.

She was rushing about the room. Whatever she needed to take care of must have been important.

Either way, I was not comfortable staying in that house. I didn't know her grandmother.

"I'll come with you," I replied, getting up from the oversized chocolate brown sofa.

"No, chill here. I will be right back."

Right as she said that, I heard another set of footsteps coming out from the back room. It was grandma Pam.

She was fussing at Danielle for coming to her house and bringing me into her house.

I could not see her yet, all I heard was her feet sticking to the floor as she walked, just as my shoes had done when I walked through the house. I felt uncomfortable among other things. I had no idea what I had done to this lady ,but I was ready to get out of her house.

Danielle had ignored the bickering of her grandmother and had bolted out the front door. As she scurried away, she yelled over her shoulder; I'll be right back A.J."

"I don't know why this girl brought chu' here" She mumbled. "I'm going to go on and have my grandson Brandon take you on home."

She yelled for her grandson to come out front to the living room. He took his time walking from the back of the house to the living room where we stood waiting for him. I was nervous. I didn't want to be out in the middle of nowhere with this man.

When he came into the room, I felt a little relieved. I had seen him before with Danielle on a few occasions. He wasn't a complete stranger.

His light-skinned complexion, nicely sculpted body with his sophisticated self.

His grandmother ordered him to take me home right away. Brandon did not seem enthused about it at all. After he got his orders, he disappeared to the back of the house one more time, and he came back dressed in some blue jeans and a navy t shirt and asked politely if I was ready? Yes I replied , and we headed out the door.His grandmother watched us leave and closed the door once we had crossed the street. Brandon didn't have a car, so we walked.

We stopped at a convenience store on the corner and talked for a bit. He said Arianna, "I have had a crush on you since I first met you ,I think you're, cute, and you have a very fine shape ." He looked at me with a pleased smirk. Brandon confessed to me that he had a crush on me again , and he had asked Danielle to arrange it so that we could hang out. They had set the whole thing up, but they didn't count on their grandmother Pam being at home.

Though, I was flattered by his interest in me; I asked him how was I getting home and was daniella still taking me shopping ? He said what about what I just told you am only fourteen, I am just ready to go home I said . He looked at me like that's it nothing else to say ? I want to know "Is Danielle gonna' be back anytime soon to pick me up?"

He could tell that I was afraid. Arianna, I'm going to get you home, trust me".

"He said let's go back to the house and he will call Danielle and tell her she needs to come back now and pick you up, is that alright?" yes I replied".

His tone was calm and reassuring. I was once again relieved. Just as he said, we walked back to his grandmother's house. He led me into the same room with the oversized sofa and had me sit there while he went to the back to use the phone. His grandmother was not pleased to see me back in the house again.

"Girl whatcha' doing back here? She questioned. "Didn't I tell Brandon to take you home?"

I was about to answer when Brandon darted out from the back to my rescue.

"Yes ma'am, you did. I just got off the phone with Danielle, she's gonna' come back and pick AJ up."

My sense of relief had vanished. I didn't know why this lady was so unhappy with me being there. I needed to get out of her house, and quickly.

"Danielle ain't picking nobody up from here at my house. She ain't welcomed here. That girl ain't nothing but trouble."

Her voice was raspy and harsh sounding. Her tone wasn't mean, but it was very curt and dry. Whatever Danielle did to get on her grandmother's bad side had to be bad. Her grandmother

was not happy with her at all. As I stood there trying to make sense of the matter, Ms. Pam started to ask me all types of questions.

She wanted to know why I wasn't in school, and if my dad knew where I was, and who I was with; she even urged me to call him and have him come to get me.

I was nervous by the end of her interrogation. I wanted to get out of there, and back to safety. I told her how Danielle was supposed to be taking me shopping, and she laughed at me and said: "that ain't happening". She said AJ you should not be around that girl she no good.

She said to me that Danielle has no job and she was a thief that owed her money. By that time, I had heard enough. I called my house, but there was no answer. I had no idea what to do. I had no money, and no one knew where I was.

***

Ms. Pam yelled out for her grandson, who had left us in the living room and disappeared again somewhere in the house. When he came into view, she instructed him to get on the bus with me and take me home. She even gave him the money to get us there and get him back. I was so over all the drama that had taken place.

I said my goodbyes once again to Ms. Pam. Brandon and I headed back out towards the bus stop. We took the same route as before, only this time we walked past the convenience store and passed the bus stop.

"Where are we going?" I asked.

He stopped his stride in front of me and turned around. He seemed a bit winded, as he should've been. We were walking up an incline, and he was walking like he was in a rush. As much as I wanted to get home, I wasn't even walking that fast.

He told me that Danielle was going to pick us up at the mall, but we have to meet her there.

I wasn't sure that I believed him, so I asked what mall and I asked if he could let me borrow a quarter to use the payphone.

He started to walk again as if he didn't hear me ask him these questions.

"We're gonna' call her once we get to where we're going. No need in wasting time calling now."Arianna, trust me I'm going to get you home," said Brandon.

I let the issue go, and kept on walking. We passed by several more bus stops on our way, so I don't know where we were. I whined and asked if we could jump on the bus, but he said "No" he have someone coming to pick us up.

I guess he was trying to save the money that his grandmother gave him to put me on the bus. I didn't see anything wrong with saving the cash if someone could take me home where I wanted to be.

***

Downtown Atlanta is where we ended up. I had no idea it was possible for me to walk that far. The longer we walked, the more I whined and complained to be taken home. Brandon had been ignoring my pleas the entire way, up until now.

"Would you hush up!" he yelled. "I'm gonna' getchu home." Your grandmother gave you the money to take me home just use it Mr. Cheapskate. It was apparent that I had finally struck a nerve. We had passed yet another bus stop. The school day had come and gone. I had no idea what time it was exactly, but it seems to be late in the day. The sun was almost setting.

I just want to go home now.

I was tired of being yelled at, so I stopped asking about how was I going to get home. I guess that worked to my advantage because we had finally stopped walking. We had stopped at a local corner mart, and Brandon told me wait outside while he went in. I could see him through the dirty glass door of the shop. He was talking to a guy and pointing over his shoulder at me.

Whatever they were talking about, I knew I was involved.

I was anxious to know what the conversation was about; It didn't take long for Brandon to come back outside to me. He swung the door of the store opened and told me that he had gotten us a ride. Brandon words were music to my ears all I wanted was to get home. Staying out late was not normal for me, especially without my parent's permission.

"Is this the ride you were telling me about?" I asked.

I wanted to know if they knew each other, or if he had just asked some random stranger to take me home. His reply was short and laced with a grump.

"Yeah."

The feeling was mutual. I was just as over Brandon as he was over me.

We stood there waiting for this man that look like a black cowboy to come out of the mart for about five minutes. My stomach was making all kinds of noise. I was hungry and thirsty.

I hadn't eaten anything since friday morning breakfast, it was late and dark. I just wanted a shower, a meal, and my bed. I wanted to be home.

Once we got in the car, nobody was talking, I ask brandon do this man know where I stay? he did not respond to me. So I said "where are y'all taking me? Brendon said to meet Danielle. It seemed like we had been riding forever. I was doing my best to stay awake on the ride, but I had fallen asleep.

I knew that I did because I remember black cowboy driving up to the old, raggedy, wooden house on a hill, but I didn't remember what route we took to get there. Black cowboy had parked the car, and before he could turn off the motor, I had jumped out. I was ready to see Danielle so that she could take me home.

We got to the front door of the house, and Brandon knocked on the door. His knock was weird. It was not the average door knock, but more of an off pattern, distinctive knock—like a password type sound. Immediately the door swung open, and he took my hand and pulled me into the house behind him. He had taken me to this room and told me to stay put. The last time I did that, I ended up left at Ms. Pam. I was nervous and scared. I didn't want to stay put; I wanted to go home.

Brandon disappeared from the room.

There was a lot of commotion and music going on in the house so I couldn't tell which way his footsteps took him. I tried to listen intently, but between my racing heartbeat, the music playing and the numerous voices coming from different directions of the house, I could not decipher anything.

I was sitting in a small wooden chair in what seemed to be the kitchen when this old lady walked in. She looked to be sixty-years-old. She was a darker complexion than me. Her hair was a bluish-gray, and she smelled like cinnamon.

"You, a pretty lil thing, ain't chu."

Her voice was pleasant. It reminded me of my middle school teacher, Mrs. Cassie. Her tone was enough to calm my nerves just a little. I was grateful to see another individual. I wanted to ask if Danielle was there.

"Stand up so I can take a good look atcha'." She said while holding her hands together like a frame. I wasn't sure why she needed me to stand, or why she wanted a better look at me. I was a mess. My red blouse was stained with powdery white stains, from my sweat from all that walking we did. My jeans skirt were slightly discolored too. My neat ponytail had been long gone. Strands of my brown hair were wildly tossed all over my head and face.

Despite all that, I decided to stand up. I didn't know this lady or what she was capable of, so I didn't want to cause any trouble or risk getting kicked out of the middle of nowhere.

"Oh yeah," she said with a grin. "You can make lots of money."

"Huh?" I was confused. "Lots of money."

It was beyond time to go. I was no longer comfortable with this old lady being in the room with me. I began fidgeting with the collar of my blouse. I was at a new level of discomfort. I guess the way I was feeling became evident because she extended her hand towards me, and told me her name.

"Around here they call me Cinnamon."

She did a twirl as if she was on the catwalk modeling. Knowing her name made sense to why she smelled like cinnamon. She smelled like a bakery. Her introduction made me feel calm again. I didn't give her my name; I just told her it was nice to meet her acquaintance.

Cinnamon offered me something to drink, and I gladly accepted. Thank you, Ms. Cinnamon, I was so thirsty. No need to call me Ms. Cinnamon I ain't that old. I guzzled down the can of pop she gave me; she asked me a series of questions. She wanted to know who I was there with, and why I was on this side of town. I answered all of her questions. I told her I was with Brandon, and how he was taking to meet Danielle so that I can get home. She followed up with asking me why I was in such a hurry to get home. I told her that I needed to get home because my parents will be concerned about me and its church tomorrow.

"Oh, so you're one of dem good ole church girls? How'd you end up running with Danielle and dem?"

That question made me just as nervous as when Ms. Pam had told me about Danielle, and why she didn't want her around. They must be awful people. My mind was racing with a series of questions. I, however, shook myself free from the mind racing to answer Cinnamon's questions. I told her that Danielle was a friend of the family. I didn't want to give her too much information, just in case Danielle owed her something. I didn't want to be held liable for payment because she was my cousin.

It seemed as if Cinnamon had gotten all the information she needed. She got up from the table we had ended up sitting in the kitchen, and she headed towards the archway from what I could see, that looked like the living room, with some sort of hallway.

The vibrancy of her bluish-gray hair became faint the further down the hall she got.

The music in the house was still playing, but it was lower than when I first came into the house.

A door had opened. The loud creaking sound that echoed from the hallway made that evident. Shortly after, there was a slam of a door, and lots of chatter and yelling. Cinnamon had gone back there and started a ruckus with whoever was at the back. Before long, I saw the black cowboy and two other men appear from the hall from my seat in the kitchen, It was dark in the hall so you couldn't see exactly who was coming towards me until they got to the archway. I could tell that was black cowboy because of his hat he had on, not sure who the other men was.

There was still fussing going on. This time around, it sounded like two females. Cinnamon's voice was distinctive, so I knew which was hers. The other one sounded like Danielle I sprung up from my seat and headed towards the living room area, to go down the hall. I needed to see her; I needed to demand that she take me home right now. Before I could make it down the hallway, Cinnamon was on her way back to me. She asked me again who it was I was waiting for, and how I had gotten there.

I wasn't sure if she had memory issues, or if she didn't hear me the first time, but I told her again.

Brandon "brought me here because Danielle is going to pick me up, and take me home," I replied frantically.

"She was supposed to pick me up on Friday, but it's now Saturday, and I have no idea where I am." I continued.

I needed her to hear the desperation in my voice. I just had to get to Danielle She rested her hand on the side of my face, and kissed my cheek.

"It's gonna' be alright shuga. We gon' getcha home."

Cinnamon had me wait in the living room while she went back down the hall. I wanted to see what was going on and make sure that if Danielle was back there, she could see me when she came out of the room. I went to the kitchen and drug the chair I had sat in earlier into the living room by the archway. I sat and waited. The music still played, and for over an hour there was no sign of Cinnamon, Danielle, or Brandon. I wondered what was going on down the hall. It was uncanny to me that none of the people that I had spoken to was anywhere in sight.

Finally, I heard the creak of a door, and footsteps shortly thereafter. As I watched intently, I noticed flickers of blue, and what seemed like white getting closer and closer in sight. It was Cinnamon. Her slender, soggy frame appeared before me in the archway where I was sitting. She had changed clothes too. When I first saw her she was wearing a blue floral print house dress, with the metal buttons down the middle; now she had on a dusty, tattered looking burgundy robe halfway tied around her waist.

She looked like she had fallen asleep, and had a bad nightmare or something. Her hair was a mess, and she was sweaty looking. I knew she hadn't taken a shower, because her makeup was still on and all smudgy looking.

"That Brandon fellow said he's gonna come talk to you. Just hold on a minute."

She had that grin on her face from earlier when she told me to stand up. I didn't know what was going on, but I knew I wanted Brandon to hurry up. Cinnamon turned around and left me standing at the archway waiting. She had walked back down the hall, where I could not see where she went exactly. I just heard the open and close of a door. I took a seat and waited to hear the door again, in hopes that I would see Brandon or even Danielle.

My wait wasn't long. I heard a door open, but it didn't close. Heavy thuds were made on the floor, and I knew whoever it was, was a male. With as many people as I had already seen come through the house since I was there, I did not know what to expect. Luckily for me, it was Brandon.

"Yo A.J., It's late. So, we are going to sleep here tonight, and we will take you home in the morning...alright?"

Although what he said sounded like a question, the look on his face told me it was rhetorical. I was not happy. I repeatedly said that I wanted to go home. I wanted to see Danielle I whined about how she was to take me home, and if he just let me call my mom, she would come to get me. He did not budge. He told me nah it's too dangerous. He even made matters worse by telling me that Danielle wasn't there yet, and she would be there in the morning.

I was tired of being lied to by everyone. How would Brandon know that Danielle was coming in the morning if they didn't have a phone there? I needed to use a phone. I needed to let my mom know that I was okay. Tears streamed down my brown cheeks. I was filled with emotions of anger, abandonment, and fear. Brandon wasn't moved by any of it. While I whined and begged to use the phone, he had told me that I was not going home. The look he gave me insinuated that I may never go home.

He took my hand and led me down the dark hallway that everyone seemed to be mysteriously appearing from the darkness. As I walked down the hall, all I could see were doors. It was almost 10 doors down the hall. They were all one next to the other, on both sides of the hall. We stopped at the last door on the right, and Brandon told me to go in. I didn't want to, but he stood behind me, blocking any route I would have to run around him. I decided not to fight, so I walked in and stood against the wall.

Chuckling softly, he said, "you might wanna go ahead and get comfortable, cause this were you sleeping tonight."

I didn't have time to respond. Brandon closed the door in my face. The tears did not stop. My watery eyes made it hard to take in the space I was in. All I could see were two windows with thick bars on them. The only light in the room came from the moonlight. There was no way for me to escape. Tears rushed from my eyes even more. I crouched down to the floor holding my stomach because it was aching with pain. It was a pain I had never felt before. It was as if my soul was ripping inside of me.

The door opened, and Brandon came in and a pillow and a blanket on the floor then he walked right back out. I know they weren't concerned about me. I knew who was concerned, so I talked to him.

"God, what have I done? I'm sorry about this, please forgive me." I prayed. "I shouldn't have wanted pants so bad, that I lied to go get them. Jesus, please forgive me help me get out of this!"

On the other side of the closed door to the room, I could hear the voices of two men talking as if I was in the hall with them.

"C'mon man! Let me put her on the corner. I'll give you a good deal."

By this time, I was cradling myself in a ball on the floor. My tears were so torrential that a puddle had formed under my head. Who they were referring to, I didn't know for sure, but everything within myself was saying that it was me. The door opened, and the voice of one of the men I overheard in the hallway asked me why I was crying. I answered by telling him that I wanted to go home.

"You can come home with me."

I told him no. I exclaimed that I wanted to go home to my family, and he replied by telling me that he could be my family.

"Nigga, what you doing in here?"

I knew that voice; it was Brandon. He started cussing at the guy that was trying to take me home and pushed him out the room. He slammed the door shut, and the guy banged on it, yelling.

"I just wanted to test her out!"

At that moment, for the first time since we got to that house, I felt like Brandon had my best interests at heart. He told me that Danielle had been at the house earlier that day and that she was going to be back in the morning to take me home.

He was treating me nice again; he wasn't yelling or fussing at me. He started acting like the guy I met, that said he had a crush on me.

Brandon sat on the floor across from me in one corner. I was sitting up in another corner talking to him.

"Uhm...are you sure I'll be going home tomorrow? Cause my parents will be worried about me and, I've gotta get to church."

He laughed aloud for the first time since we met.

"Yeah, I'm sure. You've said it tons of times."

I didn't know why he found that to be so funny. I was serious. I ask Brandon what time was it, he just left out ,he came back with a clock sit it on the floor. Sleep had finally gripped me, and I was losing the battle of giving in to it. The clock radio across the room read 3:20 Am, in big red numbers I was exhausted, and Brandon knew it. He laid a blanket that he had brought in earlier on the floor next to him and put the pillow on top.

"Come get some sleep. By the time you wake up, it'll be time to take you home."

***

The room was drafty. There was no furniture or curtains to help break the chill in the air. As I tried not to fall asleep. I laid on the blanket wide awake, staring at the window thinking how can I get out of here. I must've nodded off to sleep because Brandon was laying on the other side of the blanket, breathing heavily. It seemed like he had no trouble at all.

I rocked back and forth in my spot on the blanket. My rocking must've been too much because Brandon's hand was on my lower back. I thought he was asleep, but it was possible that my moving around woke him.

"I'm sorry, I didn't mean to wake you," I whispered.

He told me that I didn't wake him and that he needed something to help him go to sleep. I did not know what he was referring to, and I didn't want to know. I apologize again for moving around so much and told him that I would not move. I was still to the point where he couldn't tell if I was breathing. I did not want to make another move, in fear of what could happen.

Brandon nudged me and whispered, "Aye, AJ are you sleep?"

I did not answer him. I stayed still, hopefully he would think that I was asleep. He asked again if I was sleeping, and I laid there not saying a word or making a move. I never wanted to be home with my family so much in my life. All I wanted was for daylight to come and this nightmare to be over.

I felt tears well up in my eyes again. I was very nervous. I laid still and held my tears back. The room was quiet again. Brandon was no longer asking me questions or nudging me, so I allowed my body to relax. The moment I did that, I felt his hands go under my blouse.

I shot up from the floor and began yelling at him not to touch me. He yelled back at me telling me to calm down, and that he was only checking to see if I was cold because the room was so drafty. I assured him that I was not cold, and told him that I did not want to be touched. He assured me that he was only checking on me and that he would not touch me again.

Hesitantly, I laid down on the blanket again. This time I made sure to move further away from him to the point where I was laying more on the bare floor, than the actual blanket. By the time I finished repositioning myself, Brandon had moved he was wide awake sitting in the corner facing me. His eyes seem to be glowing . With the darkness of the room surrounding us, his eyes looked scary. He started threatening me. He told me if I didn't give him a kiss that I would not get home to my family. I begged him not to touch me, and I told him that I didn't like kissing. He told me to shut up. I tried to fight him off but, There was no strength in me to fight him off. I laid there crying, praying that God would help me. There was nowhere for me to run. I didn't know where I was or who would try to snatch me once I got out the door.

"I'm gonna have sex with you."

I was confused. I didn't know if I was to say something back or not say anything at all.

"Why have sex with me? I'm just a young girl. You're in your twenties, I reminded him again I'm only fourteen." I told him that I heard that older men that slept with young girls went to jail.

He didn't take to kindly to that fact. He said A.J. if you say anything, you might come up missing. He pinned me down, and I laid there. I laid there scared, crying, and praying for the nightmare to be over.

All because of the decision I made.

PAMELA TUCKER

CHAPTER TWO:

─────── ❧❧❧ ───────

MY WORLD HAD SHIFTED

Morning! It had finally come to rescue me from the imprisonment I was held captive in overnight. The room filled with sunlight as I laid in a ball on the floor of the room in a corner. The events of the night played over in my head. I remember Brandon rolling off of me within a matter of minutes, and going straight to sleep. I remember hearing within myself, that everything would be okay. That was ironic to me. There was no way that things would be okay. How was what I was enduring okay!

Coming out of my daze, the tears flowing I wiped my face with the palm of my hand and got up from the floor. I felt gross. I needed a shower. I got dressed and sit in a corner and waited for that scum to wake up. I didn't want to wake him in case he would try to hurt me again. My wait for him to wake up was not long. He rustled around a little and then got up on his feet.

He looked at me and said "You look like you've been up all night."

He was grinning like the Cheshire cat from Alice in Wonderland. He pulled up his jeans, and said, "That's the best sleep I've had in awhile."

There was nothing I could say to him—nothing I wanted to say.

"Oh, so you mad now huh?"

He could care less about how I was feeling. He got what he wanted.

"You lucky I like you because we could make some good money with you ."They were planning to pimp me out. Once he got dressed, he grabbed my hand and told me to come because it was time to go. We walked down the hall, and straight through the archway. No one was in sight. The house was like a ghost town. We got outside, and to my surprise, there was the black cowboy. He was leaning against his car as if he was waiting for us to come out.

I got in the car, and Brandon, the black cowboy, and two other guys got in with us. I was afraid not know what they were going to do with me. Their conversation was a back and forth quarrel about why they weren't taking me to the spot. I did not know what the spot was, but Brandon kept telling them that something came up and the plan had changed.

I was too sleepy and in far too much pain to ask any questions about what they were talking about. I needed all my energy to stay awake so that I could make sure I got home safely. Before long we were on the highway passing the Stagecoach exit, on our way to my house. Brandon had told the black cowboy where I lived when I got in the car.

***

"Man, you can't drop this girl off right in front of her house!"

One of the guys that had gotten in the car was talking to black cowboy. After a few seconds of silent contemplation, he drove around the corner and parked. The car was left running. I was anxious to get out. If I was by the door, I would have already jumped out of the car, but I was sitting between Brandon and some other guy.

They both looked me up and down, and then Brandon opened the door and got out.

"You just gonna let that money walk? man you crazy."

That was the first time since meeting him that I heard black cowboy talked. His voice was raspy and thick. Out of all the guys I had seen that night, he was clearly the oldest of them all. He was a grown man, from the looks of his full beard and thick mustache, he was well into his forties. Brandon was blocking my exit from the car. He went back and forth quarreling with the other guys about why he was letting me go. He told them that he knew my parents, and he had to make sure I got back.

Finally! Their exchange of words stopped, and Brandon moved to let me out of the car.

"Arianna, I promise if you ever say..."

Before he could finish his statement, I told him that he did not have to worry. I was not going to tell anyone what had happened.

"Good! Cause, I may not come back for you, but they will."

He got back in the car and closed the door. They began to pull off and he rolls up the window while mouthing "I'm sorry." I hustled home, making sure not to run because I was afraid that they would see me running and think I was going to tell someone. I took my time and walked around the corner, and up the hill to my house. I wasn't too far from getting there when Sabrina came out of her house running toward me.

Frantically saying "AJ, where have you been? Yo momma has been looking for you." Sabrina's hands were flailing about like she was an irate mom fussing at her child.

"Look, it's a long story, but I can't talk now. I've got to go."

I left her standing there. I didn't want to risk her asking me more questions or figuring out what had happened. As I walked away I heard her ask if I was okay, and she said I looked like I hadn't slept in days. I just kept walking, at home was where I wanted to be.

When I got to the house, I was prepared to walk in, go straight to the bathroom to take a shower, and go to bed. Once I had opened the door and got inside, the furthest I could walk was to the chair in the living room. The events of those days played out in my head as I sat there. I was filled with multiple emotions all at once. Madness, embarrassment, outrage regret, frustration, and self-hatred, sadness, shame, guilt were dominating my heart.

"Arianna Jay! Where have you been?" My mom's voice rang in my ears.

It was not the hushed, whisper-like tone I was used to. It was evident that she was upset and concerned. My dad came out of the room. He began his typical rant about how absurd I was, and how much trouble I gave them.

"You need to get rid of her. She crazy and hard-headed." He interjected.

My mom shot an ice cold look at him and said "Tucker with love and kindness have I drawn thee. She then turned back to me and told me if I ever did anything like that again, that she would have to get me some help for runaway teens. The only thing I could muster up was a nod of the head to let her know I understood. She was asking me so many questions but I didn't know how to answer them. My mind was not in the moment with them. It was constantly replaying the events of the night like a movie reel at a horror show. I wanted this conversation to be over just so I could shower and go to bed.

There was no way I was going to tell my family what happened. I didn't feel close to them like that. Besides my family didn't come together unless they wanted something from the one they were coming to see. I often wondered why I was in the family I was in. Internally, I fought with whether I should say anything or not to them about what happened. I envisioned possibly telling the police, but I knew because of my age, they would have to tell my parents. So, I quickly scratched that idea. Briefly, I thought about my aunt Karen. I talked to her about lots of things, but never about something this serious.

The thoughts were becoming far too much for me to contain. The more I thought about who to tell, and what I would be telling, the more I felt emotions well up in me. I excused myself and got up from the chair I was sitting in. I needed to get out of there. As I made my way to my room, all I could think of was how much I suffered through, all because of the decision I made just to go shopping for some pants. Just as time past, my world had yet again shifted.

***

Only two and a half weeks before my 15th birthday, and I don't feel well. Nothing I ate or drank was staying down. It had been Two months since I had been raped, and along with the emotional pain, I was now suffering physical pain. The thought of being pregnant plagued my mind. I didn't know much about that just what I heard from the school. My family didn't talk about things like sex, drugs, pregnancy, life. I did not want to believe that I was. I could only imagine what my family would say. Being an almost fifteen-year-old mother was not what I was expected of me. I knew that an abortion was out of the question, but besides that, I had no clue what to do.

I went to the only one I could talk to. I fell on my knees and talked to God. Once I had prayed, I picked up the phone and called my aunt Karen. I spilled my guts and told her everything except about the rape. Finally! I had told someone little of what I had gone through. I was hoping that I would start getting better, but that was a faint hope.

My aunt had told my sister Myra I was pregnant and to take me to the doctor. The next day Myra took me to the clinic, to find out if indeed I was pregnant, and I was. Driving home, she did not say a word to me. The ride was silent from the time we left the clinic until the time we got home. Once we got into the house, she immediately asked my mom to have a seat she told my mom.

"AJ is pregnant."

Myra words were supportive also lace with compassion and concern in her voice. There was no delay in response from my parents. My mom words were not really said but shown. My dad, he was his regular old negative self when it came to me. He said I got what I deserved.

***

The entire family was summons to my mom's house that evening. They all sat around talking about how much of a whore I was. I was even called a dumb slut. They came together to figure out what I should do. My mom did not say anything at that time. She just looked at me with such disappointment. Everyone kept spewing their venomous words at me. None of them knew that a twenty-two-year-old man had raped me. I doubt that they would even care. They were all sure that I got what I deserved because I was out being a hot tail.

"Okay now. Y'all need to quit with all the name calling."

My brother-in-law got up from his seat across the dining room table to defend me. I don't know if he knew what might have happened to me , but whatever provoked him to speak up on my behalf, I was grateful.

His baritone voice was calm, yet stern. "None of us know what this child is going through, or whatever happened to get her in this situation."

The room calmed immediately. It was as if they were taking in his words, and considering what he had said. No one uttered another word. Quietly they sat around the room, looking at one another.

Finally, it was over—not really. My brother Junior got up from his seat and rushed me. Before he could get to me, my dad and brother-in-law, Patrick stopped him before he could hit me.

His skinny hands were flailing about. He was yelling and fussing, telling me that I made our mom sad. He was filled with lots of anger about what I had done.

Patrick and my dad drug Junior out of the house, and onto the porch.

"How could you do this AJ! Why would you do this to us!" He yelled.

I didn't know what to say. There was nothing I could say at that moment to make him any less angry. All of this for a few pairs of pants. I went to my room tears begin to flow again.

CHAPTER THREE:

——————— ❧❧❧❧❧ ———————

TEEN MOM

The verdict was in, abortion was not an option and neither was adoption. My family had planned life out for me for the duration of my pregnancy. My mom got her request granted too, I stopped going to church. The only reason that happened was that I decided that staying at home was better than being gawked at during the entire service.

The house was only a little better than going to the church. I didn't have to worry about being looked at all day, my situation there was being overlooked while I was there. My dad continuously stated I got what I deserve, and none of my siblings really spoke to me about how I felt about everything. They all were married and had their own families.

My mom, she didn't look at me long, every time she did, all I saw was eyes filled with disappointment.

School! Yet another place that my face became forbidden from. People looked at me funny, and most of the kids whispered and made their jokes, but those weren't the reasons leading to me deciding to stay home. I was constantly sick throughout the pregnancy.My blood levels were low, and I had to take shots and medication multiple times a day. It was in my best interest to not go to school.I was fine with the decision too.

My friend Sabrina brought my school work home for me, so I didn't have to worry about falling behind in class. She was my best friend.

"So, don't kill me...but who's the daddy?" Sabrina asked.

She had come over to bring my books, and other assignments over. In all the months of her coming over, she had never asked me any questions about being pregnant. It was one of my favorite things about her; she never intruded on my privacy, she always waited for me to tell her what I wanted her to know. Today was different though. She wanted to know why

I didn't tell her I was having sex, and who I was having it with. She knew just about everything about me.

I was leery about telling her, Sabrina was a nice girl, but she had a temper on her. I attempted to ignore her questions by asking for the instructions for my school work, but she asked me again. The last thing I wanted was to lose a friend, especially when everyone else around me had chosen to shun me, so I decided to tell her—not before making her promise that she would not tell anyone else.

Sabrina promised to keep her mouth shut, and I told her everything. I told her how Danielle was to take me shopping, and how she had set me up to meet her cousin Brandon. I told her how I ended up in the middle of nowhere, meeting a whole bunch of strange people, and how I was raped, I kept saying no no no and pleading for him not to do me like that, and they wanted to turn me into a prostitute. I give her the short version of what happened ,She was furious. Sabrina started pacing the floor of my living room and fussing which she has never done in my house. She started making threats about hunting Danielle down and finding out who and where Brandon was. She wanted to avenge me.

"Sabrina, would you calm down! This is not good for my baby."

I was rubbing my stomach, and trying to keep myself from getting motion sickness from watching Sabrina walk back and forth. I appreciated the fact that someone was finally on my side, but I didn't want any more violence around me.

Regardless of how it all happen, That part is over I have a baby inside of me that I love and I have to think about my child now. That did the trick, she had calmed down and took a seat next to me.

Sheila had walked in on us sitting in the living room. Sabrina took her presence as her cue to leave. I walked her to the front door and thanked her for bringing my work. I closed the door and headed to my room.

I sat in my room alone talking to my stomach. It was no surprise that I was alone because since I got pregnant that was my fate. What surprised me though was Sheila coming into my room to sit with me. I loved my siblings but, Sheila she was like a second mom to me.

She had taken a seat on the corner of the bed, right above my feet. Sheila didn't hold any punches, she asked me who the father was. That seemed to be the question of the day. I had already put some of the truth out there, so I told her the name, and even about how I met him. I didn't tell her that he raped me, but I told her everything else.

She got angry and told me that she would be right back. It was just her and I in the house. Our folks were at church. I heard Sheila stomping across the floor in the living room, and within a few seconds, her pace stopped. I got up to see what she was doing. By the time I had made it down the hall and into the living room, I could hear her on the phone.

"You no good jerk..."

"Sheila!" I yelled. "Who are you talking to?"

She had called Danielle's grandma's house looking for Brandon. She wanted to give him a piece of her mind and let him know that he needed to take care of his responsibilities. He had to have said something crazy because Sheila had lost it. She was fussing and carrying on over the phone. I could not believe it, she was standing up for me too. She gave off another few words and then hung up the phone. She took a deep breath and then came over to me.

"What did he say I asked?"

My eyes were filled with tears and wonder. I was curious to know what Brandon had said to ruffle her feathers so much.

"That no good jerk said that it ain't his baby."

I was not surprised. Why would I be surprised at what he had done to me? For him to own up to it would have been more of a shock to me than what he did. Brandon was no good, and he made it clear that he was not going to be responsible for the life of his child, and I was relieved by it.

***

"Momma !"

I was yelling in pain. I needed to go to the hospital. I started to feel sharp pains earlier that week, but they always easy up. Tonight was different. It was Sunday night, and the pain would not go away. When my mom finally came to see about me, I asked her if she could take me to the hospital. She told me that my dad would take me. As soon as the words rolled off her tongue I heard my dad's voice echoed through the halls.

"Oh no, I'm not. Get one of her sisters, or her lil friends to take her. But I ain't"

"Tucker Dobbins!"

"Well since we are calling names, Marilyn Dobbins!"

"Tucker, would you quit being childish and take her to the hospital."

"I said, I ain't taking her."

I watched as my parents fussed back and forth about taking me to the hospital. I wondered who would give in first. As usual, my mom gave in and ended the argument by picking up the phone and calling the ambulance. I was hunched over in pain. My labor pains had started and I didn't even know it.

The ambulance did not take long to get to the house. Once they got there it took another twenty minutes before we could leave because no one wanted to ride in the ambulance with me. The EMT told them that I couldn't ride alone because I was a minor. My parents started their back and forth toss of responsibility again until my mom finally gave in. She asked EMT if she had to ride with me in the back because she didn't want to, my mom got up front, and we were on our way.

The ride to the hospital was quick. They must've run every stop light there was on the way there. When we got to the hospital I had to be walked in. The pain of it all was excruciating. My mom followed behind us, but she walked as if she didn't want to be there. She was walking slow.

Once I had gotten checked in, and placed in a room, the doctor came and to check how far I had been dilated.

"Oh wow! She is far ahead, it's time for her to push."

Everyone sprang into action. The nurses and the doctor worked to get me ready for my baby to come. They held my feet and my hands and told me to push. I pushed with all my strength, and it was barely any in me. I was tired before I had even gotten there , I had been in labor for 4 days but did not know it. They kept telling me to push, and I kept telling them that I couldn't. The nurse said I only needed one more, the big one, so I took a deep breath in, and pushed.

My baby had come and she was 5lbs 12oz and 21in long. I was grateful to God for my beautiful baby girl regardless of all I had to go through. I love my baby girl.

I was moved to the recovery room, and my mom was invited to go with me. She did not take the invitation.

"I have to head downstairs, someone is on their way for me." She said bitterly. "Don't bring no more babies in my house."

She left out. It was the harshest I had ever remembered her talking to me—to anyone really.

Marilyn Dobbins was always sweet, and stern when she had to be. This time her tone was different. There was no sweet or no stern, it was just disappointment and hurt. Before she walked out I told her that she and the baby had the same complexion alike, and even asked her if she had gotten the chance to see her. She told me no. In her eyes, I could tell that she didn't want to, so I let her leave.

My mom had been gone for ten minutes or so before the nurse walked in with my bundle of joy.

"So, what are we calling her?" she asked as she laid my baby girl in my arms.

I looked down at my daughter. Holding her was the most special and most surreal experience I had ever imagined. I looked into her pretty face and played with her beautiful light brown hair, and then it came to me.

"Carla! Her name will be Carla Tyeshay Dobbins.

My heart was filled with so much love as I held her in my arms.

"That's a beautiful name, for a beautiful baby girl."

The nurse drew the curtains back into my room to let the sunlight in, and then helped me prepare to breastfeed for the first time. She adjusted the pillows behind me and then repositioned Carla in my hands. It was amazing! I was new to it all, so the nurse had to put my nipple in Carla's mouth, but once it was there, Carla went to town.

As soon as she finished eating, Carla dozed off to sleep. The nurse came and got her, and took her to the nursery. She encouraged me to get some rest and told me that she would bring Carla back into the room for her next feeding. I was exhausted, so I took her advice and shut my eyes for a few minutes.

***

My few minutes for a nap turned into a deep slumber. By the time my eyes had opened, it was the next morning and the nurse was waking me up.

"Is it time to feed her again?"

I was ready to see my baby. I didn't intend to sleep as long as I did, but my body needed it.

"I'm sorry Arianna, but Carla was having some trouble breathing. You 're gonna' have to go to her."

My heart rate shot up. I was panicking.

"Go to her where? Where is she? How is she? What's wrong with my baby?"

Questions were flooding from my mouth like water from a fountain. I needed to know that my baby was okay. The nurse sensed my panic and hustled to get me to her. She wheeled me to the ICU where I saw Carla hooked up to machines with all kinds of tubes coming from her little body. She was not moving or making a sound. She looked helpless."Oh! My God help my baby.

Looking at her like that devastated me. I needed some answers. How could she go from being healthy and eating, to being sick, and hooked up to machines? I could not stand the sight of my baby like that. I cried out "LORD! Please Help My Baby Girl.

The nurse did her best to soothe me. She asked if I had any family that I could call to be with me, because Carla was going to need surgery.

Silently I sat trying to think of people that would come to help me through this time. I called my sister Sheila, and she told me not to worry, that she would be on the way. My next call was to Sabrina. Before I could get a word in she apologized to me for not being there when I had the baby. She said she had just found out. I stopped her in mid-speech to let her know what was going on, and that if she could come now, it would be more than enough. She told me that she would see me later and then asked me if Brandon had come to the hospital.

Brandon was the last person on my mind. I didn't call him to tell him anything. The last time his name was even mentioned was the night he and Sheila got into it over the phone. Sabrina asked for his number, and I gave it to her. I was tired of fighting, but if she wanted to waste her energy going back and forth with him, I saw no sense in stopping her.My baby girl was my only concern.

I was back in my room when Brandon came busting through the door frantically.

"Where is she?" he asked.

His light bright complexion was slightly darker than I remembered. WoW, I never thought I would see him again.

"She's upstairs in the ICU."

I was surprised that he had shown up. I could only imagine what Sabrina had told him to get him down here. The nurse came back to the room to check on me, and I told her that I was okay, and asked her to take us to see Carla. We got to the ICU and Carla was more active than when I first saw her that day. Brandon looked at her and said she looked like him.

"Yeah, that's my baby." He said it surprisingly.

His response was shocking to me. I was only fourteen at the time. He knew that I was pregnant by him. I felt myself getting upset and I really try not to get angry so I knew he needed to leave .

I told him it was time to go, and we left out to head back downstairs for him to leave and I was going back to my hospital room. The nurse stayed with Carla in the ICU, and I had mustered up enough strength to walk to the elevator with Brandon. We got on the elevator, and when the door shut Brandon came closer to me.

"She's almost gone. Let's make another one." I pushed him as hard as I could my eyes filled with tears. How dare you say that bull to me about my baby. I wanted to hurt him, something told me to stop. I backed away from him The doors opened and Sabrina was front and center waiting for her chance to get on. I suppose that she had gone to my room and was told that I was in the ICU with my baby Carla.

"A.J., what's wrong?"

She saw my tears. I could not stop them if I wanted to. I told her that this no good guy standing next to me was Brandon and that he had said that my baby was about to die. Sabrina lost it. She went off cursing him and calling him all types of names trying to fight him .

Nothing that she said fazed him. He seemed to be ignoring every name she called him.

The security guard came and put Brandon out. They had overheard what I had told Sabrina. Once he was gone, We calm down, I filled Sabrina in on what the doctors had said. I told her that Carla would need surgery and that the doctors were saying that its a slim chance that she may not make it. Sabrina had to help me back to the room.

We weren't there long before Sheila showed up. She had brought me some fresh clothes and a pair of shoes. I had asked if anyone was with her, and to my surprise, she told me that Myra and my mom were in the waiting area. She told me that my mom needed something from me. My heart got light.

I was happy to know that they were there. I changed my clothes and went out to see my mom and what she needed. Her and Myra were standing in the waiting area like they didn't want to come in the room.

Hey y'all "Mom, Sheila said you wanted to see me."

She said nothing but extended her hand with a piece of paper in it. It was my check, she wanted me to sign it. My heart immediately got heavy. That was all she wanted, for me to sign my check. Myra nor my mom went to see the baby. When I asked them why my mom told me that she needed to go to the bank before it closed. I could not believe it. My baby was sick and they could not find it in their hearts to forgive me long enough to see her.

First Brandon spewed his hurtful words, then my mom and sister didn't want to see my baby. I headed back to the room, and everyone except Sabrina left the hospital. It was at that moment that I realized that I no longer had a family. There was no way they could be family because the family didn't walk out on you when things were this important. I did not want to think about it anymore. My daughter needed me, and I needed to be there for her. I took Sabrina up to see her, and when we got to the ICU she had more tubes in her than before.

Right away I began petitioning God to help my baby. The nurse had come to me and gave me an update on what was going on. The intensity was too much for me to tolerate. The nurses instructed me to go back to my room, and Sabrina made sure I got there. I had laid down on the small cot-like mattress when another nurse came in and told me that I had to be given a shot. They had drawn blood from me earlier that day and noticed that something was going on with my blood levels were dropping again. Because of what was going on with my blood, I was told that I would have to stay on to Friday when Carla was being taken to the Children's Hospital on the other side of town.

They did not want two tragedies on their hands. I was told that Carla condition was so sensitive that moving her was a risk. They brought me all types of papers to sign, half of which I had no idea what it said. The only thing I did know about that they could not legally do the operation on her until she was at least five days old, that's why they had to wait until Friday.

**

Dr. Bennett, who was the doctor assigned to Carla's case, had come in to see if I had any other questions besides the paperwork. I told him no, and that my only concern was my daughter and him helping make her well . He told me he would do his best and proceeded to ask me a few of his own questions.

"Arianna, do you have any family that you could call."

With low cast eyes and a saddened tone, I replied, "yeah, but we're not on good terms at this time but I will try and call them."

His face said what I knew it would say. He was shocked. He asked me if I was a member of a church, and I told him that I stopped going when I got pregnant.

Dr. Bennett's shocked expression intensified. He reached into his shirt pocket and pulled out his prescription pad and a pen.

"Here, right down your name and the name of your daughter. I'll have my pastor pray for you both." His words were kind and genuine. I wrote down our names and handed him back his pen and paper. He had left me in the room by myself, and I sat on the bed staring out the window with tears streaming down my face. I felt so alone and helpless. My nurse had finally made it back to the room. She came and gave me a hug, and her eyes filled up with tears. it was as if she felt my heart. Just when I thought no one cared, and no one was there for me when the nurse hugged me,my tears flowed even more. I heard a voice say,

"I got you."

CHAPTER FOUR:

———————— ❧❦❧ ————————

DRAMA FOR THIS MOMMA

No one was going to stop me from going with my baby. It was Friday, and I knew Carla would be heading to the children's hospital at any minute. I asked to be taken up to the ICU, and I told my nurse that I was going with my baby no matter what. She continued to advise me otherwise. She told me that I couldn't properly care for my baby if I was sick myself. I was diagnosed with a severe case of anemia.

I was weak and getting weaker by the second. The nurse rushed out of the room and returned with some papers. She told me if I insisted on leaving, then I would have to sign liability waivers that stated that I left of my own free will and that the hospital, doctors, nor staff were held liable if anything happened to me once I left. I signed them and handed them back to her . I knew that God had me and that he wouldn't let anything happen to me.

I signed the papers and handed to the nurse. She took them in her right hand and helped me to my feet with the other. She was taking me up to see my daughter. When we got there Carl was being prepped for her trip to another hospital. I needed to hold her. I asked the nurse who was wiping Carla down if I could hold her, and she told me no. I could not believe her. Did she not know that I was her mother?

My nurse left my side and walked over to the rude nurse that was caring for my baby. She took her to the side and they started whispering back and forth. A few minutes passed, and the rude nurse came back to me and apologized. She told me I could hold Carla. I knew that God would work it out, so I had already taken a seat in a nearby wheelchair, and prepared myself to hold my baby.

I had to put on a face mask and a different type of hospital gown first. Immediately after I was dressed, the nurse placed Carla in my hands. I felt strength come over my body. Just holding her gave me life. I loved her so much. I knew I had to fight to get better for my baby. She opened her eyes and was staring up at me.

Holding Carla was what I needed. I stared into her face and told her that everything would be alright because God had told me that it would be. I told her that she would be going to another hospital and that I would be there with her. My nurse was so kind. She told me that she would be praying for us both.

I kissed Carla on the forehead and watched as the nurses rested her back in the clear incubator they had taken her from. I could not help but cry. That was the first time in days that I had held her. With tear-filled eyes, my nurse asked if I had any family that would come be with me. I told her that I wasn't able to reach anyone and that I would try them again.

When I got back to my room I called Sabrina and asked her if she could come by and pick me up first thing in the morning. Being the best friend that she was, she said sure thing, and asked me for the details of when, and where I needed to be where I was going. I got the details of Carla's transport from my nurse and asked

Sabrina to come and get me at 8:30 Am. She was going to take me home so that I could shower and change, and then she would drop me off to meet Carla at the hospital.

First thing in the morning Sabrina showed up. I got in a wheelchair and Sabrina and I headed up to see Carla before I left out.

"I'm sorry Arianna, but she's not here."

The nurse at the ICU entrance told me that they had taken Carla earlier than expected. Last night I was told that she would be transported at 9:00 am this morning and that the surgery would begin at noon. What happened between last night and this morning that my baby was already gone?

I was hysterical. I needed answers. The nurses told me all that they knew until Dr. Bennett came into the room. He told me that Carla's oxygen levels had dropped significantly and that they needed to move her immediately in order to save her life. He assured me that I still had time to make it to her before the surgery began He apologized for the nurse on duty not letting me know last night. I thanked him and rushed out of the hospital as fast as my feet would take me.

Sabrina did her best to calm me down. I didn't want to be calm, I wanted to be with my baby. I told her to take me straight to the hospital, but she said no because that wasn't a rational decision.

"Now A.J., you know that you're not gonna' come home until Carla does, so you need to go home and at least get some clothes. She was right, there was no sense in me going to the hospital and having to wear the same clothes if I had the opportunity to get some more clothes from home. She bobbed and weaved out of traffic and got me home quicker than I expected. I rushed into the house and grabbed as many clothes as I could manage. On my way out, I told my mom what was going on with Carla, and she didn't bat an eye or say much of anything. I did not have the time or energy to get emotional about her lack of response. I left the house and got back in the car so that Sabrina could get me to my baby.

We got to the hospital, and the nurses at the front desk of the ICU was expecting me. When I walked in I was greeted by name, and taken to meet the doctors that would be performing surgery on Carla. Dr. Bolden was the lead surgeon, and the one that told me about the procedure they would be doing. He also told me that Carla had just been diagnosed with Tetralogy of Fallot which is very rare condition only about 5 out of 10 thousands babies are born with this. Dr.Bolden told me that Carla needed to have a BT shunt tube inserted into her heart chambers to help her blood flow in the proper areas of her body. He told me that it could take three or more hours due to her age, and health, so I should be prepared to wait.

He drew a picture for me of what the tube looked like, and gave me more information on why it needed to be done. I was grateful, I finally had more information on what was going on with my baby. After he spoke to me, he directed a nurse to take me to my room. They had prepared a room for me so that I could wait for her to get out of surgery.

I ask the nurse to take me the chapel so I could pray. She took me there, and I went in and, cried my tears felt so heavy, oh God my heart is aching I ask God to give my strength and peace. I prayed and asked God to heal my baby, and make her okay. After all my pleading and asking God to forgive me , I felt a peace in my spirit, I heard the voice of God say that all would be well. So, I got up off my knees wipe my face and headed back outside to go to the room and wait. Surprisingly, the nurse was still there waiting for me. She asked if I had anyone that I wanted to call, and I did. I called my mom to update her on Carla's status. When she came to the phone, I told her what the doctors said. She said okay, and told me that she would let my sisters know.

Right as I hung up the phone Dr. Bolden came into the room. He had beads of sweat on his forehead and brows. He looked tired, and out of breath as he stood in front of me. I needed good news, and the fact that he wasn't smiling made me nervous. More than three hours had passed, but I did not complain about it. He had told me earlier that it could be more.

Before I could open my mouth to say a word, he said, "everything went well. It took longer than expected, but we wanted to take our time doing what needed to be done."

Waves of relief, joy, and peace washed over me Thank you, Jesus. I felt like I could finally release my breath. I was glad, and couldn't wait to see her.

"Thank you, doctor. Thank you! Thank you!"

Before I could bolt out the room towards the ICU, he continued with some more news.

"I must warn you that she will heal good, but from time to time, her lips may turn blue due to her Heart condition ."

***

The sight of my baby bothered me. I was expecting her to be laying in a normal baby bassinet, but she was strapped down, her eyelids were taped shut, and she was still connected to lots of tubes. The nurse that had been with me from the time I entered the hospital went to get one of the attending nurses to get me some answers as to what was going on.

I was told that they needed her to get some rest, so that's why they taped her eyes shut. They also told me that she had to be strapped down because she was moving a lot and they wanted to make sure that the stitches didn't pull apart, it was for the best at this time to help Carla get better. My heart was broken. I felt that it was my fault that this was happening to her.

As I stood there crying, the nurse that was with me was on the phone. She was talking to someone that had called looking for me.

"This is my fault. If I wasn't sick when I was pregnant with her, this wouldn't be happening."

"That's not true Arianna."

The nurse had gotten off the phone and overheard me blaming myself. She told me that my ailments during pregnancy was not the reason for Carla being sick, and encouraged me not to beat myself up.

"You should have some family here with you, maybe you want to call your family ?"

Deciding to change the subject, I asked her who was on the phone, and she told me that it was someone named Sabrina. She had called to see how the surgery had gone and if I needed anything.

"Great! Let me go call her back." I stated with a half-smile.

I didn't want to have any more conversations about my family. I was grateful that my daughter was alive, and had made it through surgery.

***

Sabrina was more than happy for me, she was there. I had called her to tell her what was going on, and she said she was going to come up to the hospital to be with me. She had become my family. I called to let my family know what was going on, and Sheila answered the phone. She told me that she had to go to work, but wanted me to keep them informed of anything else that happened.

I updated my nurse that I had talked to my family, and told her that Sabrina was on the way. She was happy that I had family come to be with me . She hugged me and prayed with me, and told me how much having loving people around me was important at this time. I was grateful for her kind words, and her prayers. Right as we had finished talking, Sabrina stormed into the room.

The first thing she did was give me a hug. My nurse left to give Sabrina and I some privacy. She asked if I had eaten, and told me that her mom said that it was important for me to eat so that I could keep my strength up.

" AJ when was the last time you ate?"

I tilted my head to the ceiling as if searching it for the answer. I was recalling the events of the past few days to determine when it was.

"Uhm, I think it was Tuesday or Wednesday."

"Are you serious!" Sabrina yelled. "AJ. it's Friday night."

Being the over protecting and caring friend that she was, she demanded that I go get something to eat. She took some money out of her pocket and handed it to me. She told me her mom was making me some food, but until that came, she was giving me some cash to make sure I ate. After bossing me around, she asked if she could see Carla.

My nurse had just walked into the room. She had overheard the question and told Sabrina that it wasn't a problem if I didn't mind. I did not mind at all. I knew that me giving the okay meant that I saw her too, so I said yes, and we made our way back to the ICU.

Upon the sight of Carla, Sabrina broke down in tears. She had to be escorted out because she was disrupting the floor with the shrill of her bawling. It was not the prettiest sight, and I knew that it was a lot for anyone to take in, so I did not fault her. I went up to her bed and held her tiny hand. I told her that everything was going to be okay, and I prayed for her. I asked God to heal her because I knew he could do it. When I finished my prayer, I let go of her hand and went to check on Sabrina.

She and the nurse were outside. She ran to me and gave me a hug.

AJ. I'm sorry. I'm so sorry."

I didn't know what she was apologizing for. She didn't do anything wrong. She wasn't the reason my baby was sick. I asked her what she was sorry for. Sabrina told me that she was sorry for me and all that was happening with Carla. I knew her heart was filled with emotion, but I needed to be strong. I was finally in a place where I wasn't crying or in tears.

"Nurse, I need to go to the chapel again."

She nodded her head in agreement and pointed me in the direction I needed to go. I told Sabrina that I would be back, and I left her with the nurse. When I got in the chapel it was just me and God. I got on my knees and I started to pray.

In the middle of my prayer for Carla, my prayers shifted and I began praying for other children and their parents. It was like an out-of-body experience. I saw myself praying for other people, and it didn't scare me. It seemed as if it was normal.

CHAPTER FIVE:

———— ❧❦❧ ————

I BELIEVE IN MIRACLES

"Carla has made a remarkable change! Her vitals are changing rapidly."

The nurse was so excited to share the news with me. I was relieved to hear what was happening. We got to the ICU, and all the nurses were hustling about taking care of Carla, and all the other babies in the room.

"I don't know what happened, they all just started getting better instantly."

Sabrina and I were brimming with joy. My nurse even jumped into the mix to help the other nurses with the babies. They took me over to Carla and told me that she was breathing on her own and that they were starting to take her off some of the machines.

"Hallelujah!"

I praised God in my heart for the miracle he had performed. Not only did he heal my daughter, but he healed many of the other babies that were with her in that room. My heart was glad. They told me that I could expect to have her with me on Monday, but she would have to stay in the ICU for the next two days for close observation. I understood their concern. They had never seen anything like it. I knew it was God. I knew that the Lord healed my baby.

The bustle around the room had settled, and parents were coming in left and right to see about their babies. One of the nurses came up to me and said Carla was a fighter.

"Yes, she is, she's my angel."

Immediately after I said that I wanted to retract it. I had no idea why I called her that. I didn't pay it too much attention. I just enjoyed the sight of my healthy baby girl. As I looked at Carla, my nurse looked at me. She was peering at me, scanning me up and down as if something was wrong. She asked if I was feeling okay, and I told her yes.

There wasn't anything wrong with me. I felt tired, but I had been going ever since I got out of the delivery room. She said she didn't like how I was looking and said that she was going to check my pressure and draw some blood. For a minute I wondered how she was going to do that because we were at a children's hospital. She must've sensed my inner thought because she informed me that they served children up to the age of nineteen. It was amusing to me that I had forgotten that I was still a child. With all the decisions I had made within the last few days, my age had escaped me.

I wasn't happy about having to give blood. When the results came back I was even less happy. I was told that my blood levels had dropped again. I needed to be up and about for my baby, not sick in bed with needles in my arms.

"Isn't there a shot or something I could take?"

Hesitantly my nurse replied, "I'll have to ask the doctor."

"No problem, I'll wait," I said

I waited for the nurse to get back. She came into the room, and shortly thereafter the doctor followed. He informed me of some shots I could take, and let me know that the shots would have to be taken at every day depending on how my blood reacted to the dosage. The nurse informed me that the transfusion was the quickest way to get me better, but I was not for it.

The doctor left out of the room to send in my prescription, while the nurse helped me get in the shower. Sabrina had left to get me something to eat. I told her I was tired, and she wanted to make sure I ate before I went to bed. She promised to bring me back something I liked.

My nurse placed a shower chair in the bathing area for me, to take my shower. She couldn't leave me in the room by myself, just in case, I fell from being weak or need help getting something. Sitting on the shower chair as I cleaned up felt great. I had been going for days and was tired. To sit and not go for a few minutes felt great.

I finished my shower, got out, and got dressed. By the time I exited the shower, I had a blanket, pillow, and bed turned down for me. Sabrina had made it back too. She went home and brought me back a plate from her mom. I thought she had gone to the cafeteria, but she told me that she wanted to go home and let her mom know the good news about Carla.

While she was there, the nurse gave me the shots. I had to take one in my buttocks. These shot were necessary because my blood was very low that it was off the charts the nurse said .

The doctor had come in and explained how bad it was after he had put in the prescription. He did it so that both Sabrina and I had a clearer understanding of how severe my condition was.

Tiredness overtook me, and I was unable to finish my meal. I had Sabrina place it in the mini fridge that was in the room, and then we both went to sleep. She had told me earlier that day that she was going to spend the night with me, and she did. She and her parents were whom I had chosen to be Carla's godparents.

They were always there for me, and Sabrina and I had been friends for years.

I got up in the middle of the night, my mind would not let me sleep. It raced with thoughts of everything, I had gone through from a childhood. I searched for the happy parts, but the dark parts seemed to surpass them. It was then that I remembered that my darkness turned to light the moment, I saw Carla's face and held her in my arms. What joy I felt, I leaned back in my bed, closed my eyes, and got the rest that I was so much in need of.

CHAPTER SIX:

———— ❧❧❧ ————

MOMMY'S LITTLE ANGEL

Sabrina had already left for the day by the time they brought Carla to me. Holding my baby girl was such a joy. I was finally able to see her and hold her without her having tubes everywhere. She was precious. There was nothing that gave me more joy than seeing her beautiful face.

It seemed like we had switched fates. I was hooked up to an IV. I couldn't move around as much as I wanted to. My vitals were still not improving. The shots I was taken had been increased to its highest dosage, and there was nothing else that I would allow to be done but to wait. I wanted to be coherent when I saw her, and all the discomfort was worth it all as I heard her faint coos, and smelled her baby scent as I held her.

***

Three weeks had passed, and I was finally on my way home with my baby girl Carla. Both she and I had been cleared by the doctor. Sabrina did me the favor of taking us home. I was glad that she could because I needed the moral support. It had been weeks since I had been home and seen my family. They had never seen Carla, they only heard about how she was doing from my phone calls ever so often.

When we got there, my mom was in the living room. She didn't say anything when I walked in with Carla. Sabrina had told a few people that she was bringing me home.

Her parents and a few of my friends from the neighborhood stopped by. I guess it was too much activity for my mom because she got up and left out of the room. I wasn't bothered too much by it. My family had made it clear that they weren't interested in being around me or my baby. I loved my baby girl, and I believed that in time, they too would love her.

Only a week of us been home my family came around they were in love with Carla. They took turns holding her and caring for her. My mom would watch her when I had errands to run. She was even okay with Carla and I going to church. I was excited about that. Everyone was so careful about how he or she handled her. Although we were free from all the doctors and nurses, I still had to monitor her. She was only 3 months and had been in the hospital ten times over that span of time. She had to have another surgery, and the doctors said that the side effect of it would be a delay in her ability to walk. I did not believe that. I knew that God was able. My baby Carla was walking at 11 mos old.

***

Carla was two years old when she had to go back to the hospital for yet another surgery. She had outgrown the valve that was inserted when she was born. I was nervous; she had undergone so much already, and I didn't know how much more she could take. The Sunday before her surgery, we went to church. I took Carla up for the pastor to pray for her he took her in his arms and he prayed even for me.

He told me to trust God. I knew that I had no other choice but to trust God, he was the only help I knew.

On the day of surgery, my family and friends and I took over the waiting room of the hospital. They did not allow me to be alone through this. They too loved Carla and wanted to make sure she was okay. The nurse took me back to the prep room, and I loved on my baby before they took her to the surgery room. She was so peaceful. I gave her kisses, before they took her back.

I was told that the surgery would be over three hours. It was three and a half hours, and still no sign of a doctor or nurse to let me know what was going on. My friends were becoming anxious as well. We all wanted to know that Carla was okay. Thankfully we did not have to wait too much longer. The doctor came out and took me to the side. He let me know that all was well, but he just took more time to make sure everything was right.

He asked me to give them another thirty minutes, and then I could come back to the recovery room to see her.

I rushed back to my family and friends and told them the good news. Everyone was happy and excited. They started making phone calls to other family and friends to let them know that all was well.

My wait was up and the nurse came to take me to the back. I was unable to hold her because of her stitches and they wanted her to be still for some hours that why she was still asleep. She had some stitches on the right side below her breastbone. Carla was still sleeping so I just stood there, holding her hand. As I took in the sight of all the tubes on her little body, the nurse instructed me that she might be able to go home tomorrow depending on her recovery. She gave me instructions on how to care for her wounds and told me that she would bring her to me. We left for home the next day.

***

"Oh my goodness! What's going on."

I had looked back at Carla she was at the table eating but she looked blue. I was frantic. I called the hospital and was told to bring her in right away. She was fine just a few minutes ago. We had just come home from the hospital two weeks ago,and everything was said to be clear.

I packed Carla in the car and raced to the hospital. When I got there, the nurses at the E.R were expecting me. I was told to wait while they took her back. Carla was crying with the nurse her, every wail, a piece of my heart broke. I felt so helpless. As I stood there in despair, the same urgency that I felt when she had to go under the knife for the first time had hit me all over again. I needed to pray. I needed God to shield and protect my baby.

I opened my mouth to pray, and immediately my heart was pricked to pray for other children and families. I did my best to fight it. I wanted all my strength and thoughts to be on Carla, but my spirit wouldn't let me. I prayed and asked God to comfort the families of the children that were ill. I asked him to heal their children, and bless each family, in the name of his son Jesus Christ.

By the time I had finished praying the nurse had come back out to me. She told me that her skin color changing was something that happened to kids with her condition. She handed me Carla and told me to make sure she got some rest when I got home. I could tell that my baby was worn out. As soon as she was in my hand, she laid her head on my shoulder.

I was a momma eagle with her that night. I didn't take my eyes off her. My sister Myra went to the store to get her medicine, and I watched Carla as she slept. Ever-so-often I put my hand on her back and her chest to make sure that she was still breathing. I did not sleep a wink that night, but my baby got the rest she needed.

***

Carla was five years old when our life shifted. When we came home from church it was about 3pm. I was so sleepy I was trying to stay awake, but I couldn't fight it, I fall asleep and had dreamt that I was in Heaven talking to an angel. The angel had told me that it was time for Carla to go back to GOD because she had done what she was sent to do. I did not pay him any attention.I was asking the angel questions. All of a sudden another voice began to speak. It came from higher above the clouds where the first angel and I was. We both looked up.

The voice said everything that would happen and what I am suppose to do and what he would do he said a nurse will call you regarding surgery for Carla. You are not to drive to the hospital, but you will have a hard time getting away, but your neighbor will take you.

When Carla goes into surgery, you will go in and out of this deep sleep. You will tell Carla, that it is okay for her to leave. For she has done what I sent here to do .I will strengthen you to do all these things."

It was the voice of God. I could not speak. I had no thoughts, I opened my mouth but nothing came out of it. My dream was interrupted by the sound of the telephone blaring. Just as in the dream the nurse from the children's hospital was on the line. They had found a donor for a heart for Carla, and wanted me to bring her in right away for heart surgery. Carla had been on that list for a long time. I was told that it would be a while before a match would be possible, but it happened sooner.

No one wanted to take us , so I called my neighbour Carla godparents to take us to the hospital and they said yes, When I got there the nurse prepped me on everything that would take place and had me sit with Carla until it was time for her to go back. The surgery wasn't taken place until Monday, but they needed her here to run some tests and prepare her body for the new organ it was about to receive.

I sat and talked to my baby about everything. The nurse had given her a shot so that she would be able to rest during their prep. Carla was far from tired. She asked to speak to everyone in the family. Her uncle Darnell was the only person that was unavailable when we called. After she spoke to everyone, we started to talk about everything. She told me how much she loved her baby sister Tyra, her Bigmama she name all her aunties and uncles, she really wanted to speak to her uncle Darnell she said she needed to tell him something. I said we will call him later. She looked at me and I looked back at her and she said love you momma. I said love you baby girl before, I could say she said that everything will be okay momma. I tried to fight back my tears I held her as tears rolled down my cheeks. I started singing Jesus loves me and she started singing with me.

I enjoyed every second with her. She was my heart's joy, my firstborn. Her medicine looked to be taking effect. Her little eyes were becoming heavier with sleep. The nurse timed it perfectly because she was on her way to get her. The nurse picked up Carla for her tests, and I gave her a big kiss and hug I let her know that I would be waiting on her.

"I love you forever, momma."

As sleepy as she looked, her eyes were still full of light and life.

"Jesus, meet my daughter, no one else."

I was shocked at the words that had left my lips. I had just given God permission to take my daughter. I immediately retracted my words. I asked God not to come for my baby girl. What am I saying she is just going for some tests she will be back soon. Almost 2 hours here comes my baby girl she was still sleeping. I kissed her and told her how much. I love her I kept rubbing her and kissing her and, telling her how much we love her. I felt so much love in my heart.

***

First thing Monday morning, Carla was taken into surgery. She was in and out of sleep they had given her some medicine , but I could tell she was scared. I kissed and hugged her and told her that we loved her, then they took her back. I was ushered to the waiting room where family and my friends had come to wait with me. I sat there for hours waiting to hear something back. Minutes went by, the hours went by and I still I hadn't heard anything yet.

I sat waiting and before I knew it this feeling of sleep had come over me. I wasn't even sleepy, but the life of me I could not stay awake. I sat in the waiting room knocked out envisioning myself floating high in the clouds. I was nudged awake by a social worker who had come to talk to me to make sure I was coping well, but I was only able to give her a few minutes of my attention before I became distracted.

The nurse that had taken Carla back to surgery was in the hall. I leaped from my seat and ran to her. I asked if everything was okay and if I would be able to see Carla now. She told me as soon as she knew something that she would come and get me.

***

Six hours and come and gone It took sixteen hours and twenty-three minutes before I heard anything about Carla. My friends and family had come, fell asleep, woke up, and left. The doctor came out and said to me that there was a complication with surgery. In the middle of the procedure, Carla had started to bleed. There were no arteries cut by mistake, she just started bleeding the Doctor said.

The doctor was terrified to tell me. His voice cracked and his eyes filled with tears as he spoke to me. Carla was in critical condition. I could feel my own heart stop beating. I needed to talk to God. I left everyone in the waiting room and headed to the chapel. I prayed and asked God why. The only answer that rested in my spirit was to trust him. I stifled my tears, got up, and headed back to the waiting room.

I was rushed with hugs and questions when I got back to the waiting area. Everyone wanted to know if I was okay. Grateful for their sentiments of care, I gave a gesture that assured them that I was fine, but my only concern was how my baby was doing. The nurse that I had rushed earlier had come to get me. I was the only one allowed back to see Carla.

The room she was in was different from the ICU. She was the only baby in that room. Carla was attached to so many tubes and machine all over again, like when she was first born. Her entire chest was left open and covered by a plastic guard due to the severity of her swelling and bleeding during surgery. She was on some strong medication, but the nurse assured me that she could still hear me.

I got close to her and squeezed her hand, and told her that I loved her. She didn't squeeze mine back.

"Nurse! I thought you said she could hear me. I just squeezed her hand, but she didn't squeeze it back."

The nurse told me to try again. I told Carla again that I loved her, and I gave her hand a light squeeze so she could know that I was there.

Carla squeezed my hand back. I was relieved. "Are there any family members that you would like to approve to see Carla?"

She had just walked in the room holding a notepad. I knew that I wasn't in the room alone just a second ago, but she was obviously not in there with me. She had just walked in. I was a little confused, I had no idea whom I was talking to that told me to do it again, but I didn't care, it had worked.

***

My heart was heavy. I could not see my life without her. I sat at Carla's bedside waiting for her to open her eyes. My family came in to see her, and everyone was asking questions. They wanted to know what had gone wrong. Three days passed by and she was not getting better. The doctor came to me and shared with me that her vitals are dropping even while she is on the heart machine, and her body is starting to reject the medicines to the point where she could feel some pain. Another doctor said that it was nothing more they could do. They said I had a decision to make. I asked him for a minute to consider all that he had said. I could say my goodbyes.

"It's okay to go, you know?"

I looked at him quizzically.

"Okay to go where?" I asked.

He looked at me and smiled, "to Heaven. It's okay to go to Heaven."

Immediately my mind went back to my dream again . His words had reminded me of what God had said to me, and I knew what it was I had to do. I went to her room and spent time talking to her and loving on her, I held her hand. One by one I allowed my family and friends to come in and see her giving them their chance to say their goodbyes.

After everyone had come and gone, I took my time to say goodbye. I told her that everyone loved her and that I will always love her and she will always be my baby girl, But I had to let her go because God loved her best. I saw a change in her breathing, it was fainter than before.

"Do you see the light, Carla ?" I asked.

My eyes were filled with tears running down my cheeks. She squeezed my hand. I told her to squeeze my hand again if she was ready to go with Jesus, and she gave my hand a tight squeeze. I knew I could no longer hold her back. I kissed her and left the room. I felt like I could not breathe, I needed a moment by myself, I sit down in a chair with my eyes closed, and I could envision Carla holding my hand. She was in perfect strength standing next to me. We were in a bright tunnel, and she was pulling me to come with her, but I told her that I couldn't go any further. I told her it's ok Jesus is waiting on her, and I let her little hand go, and watched as she walked away into the light she was smiling .

Just like that my baby was gone. I leaped from my seat and ran back to her room, holding my baby hand telling her that I and her baby sister Tyra loved her, but Jesus loves her best she squeezes my hand tight and within seconds my baby had flatlined. She was gone.

CHAPTER SEVEN:

———— ❧❧❧ ————

THE VOID IN MY HEART

The homegoing service was beautiful. Everyone that loved Carla showed up, despite what they thought of me. The minute Carla died, I went back to being public enemy number one. I was being blamed for her death. Some family and friends said that I should've gotten another doctor opinion before I let her have the surgery. Others said that I had killed my baby and that I could've made another choice. My boyfriend at the time—an atrocious man, he even made the joke about taking our daughter Tyra, so that I won't kill her too. The hurt was back. No one knew the level of pain I felt to be in this position that I was in.

I watched as my baby took her last breath and died. I was the one that had to make the decision to let her go. The Why flooded my mind I could not stand it anymore. Living in the house where she grew up became painful, I had to leave. I packed up Tyra and my things and I headed to my grandmother's house. I got there and sat on the porch, with Tyra, we both looking up at the sky I had so many questions flooding my mind. My grandmother was a sweet woman. She sat with us and said nothing, just her present was so loving and peaceful. Nevertheless the void in my heart was a pain I could not explain.

Tyra had gone to sleep my grandmother took her and laid her down.

I sit there with the why ,who, what,when,and where playing in my mind over and over and over , the void in my heart was so painful. I cried out how can I live without her.

***

I cried when I was awake, and I cried when I was asleep an ocean of tears I cried. I barely slept on my own. I took pills when I woke up and pills to go to sleep. I took pills so much that I became unfit to drive. I would swerve to the other side of the road. The thoughts of my mind tormented me. I heard voices telling me that it was my fault and that I killed my daughter. I just wanted to die. The pain was unbearable the tears I cried. I always believed that my children were to bury me, not me bury them.

***

There was no one to hear my plea, no one was around to comfort me and hear my cry. I didn't want to stay in self-pity, I wanted to be pulled out of the pain and hurt, but I couldn't find my way. I thought to myself that if I could just be free from the pain of it all, then I could learn how to live again.

God had heard me. As I sat in my grandmother's house, he told me that he would help me get through this. I questioned him about how was it possible, and he told me that I would have to learn to forgive. I had forgiven people before, but this time they had hurt me far worse than ever by, blaming me for my baby Carla's death. God told me to trust his plan because he had everything all planned out.

My tears had stopped flowing long enough for me to stand on my feet. The air around me became thin, it became difficult for me to breathe. Just the thought of forgiving people that hurt me, and saying cruel words to me and about me, and about my decision with my daughter had hardened my heart. My tears have begun to stream again.

As much as I wanted to be healed,and trust God, all I could think about was my baby my first born and the pain of it all came back to me the who, what,when,why and where . The pain of her death, caused me to live the greatest death of my soul. I can't breathe"! GOD help Me!

***

I attempted to move forward with life my mind played tricks on me. I wanted to hate people for what they had done and said to me. I continue hearing this voice that says Arianna, you have to forgive them. I ask why do I have to forgive them' they hurt me"why do I have to be the one that forgives people that hurt me? how can I forgive them when I can't even forgive myself. I want to stay right here in my grief,pain,sadness,hurt, self blame. I deserve to feel this hurt I let my baby girl die, " But it was out of my hands.

I am here at her grave again this had became my hang out place, today is different I can hear her crying for me, I am trying to dig through the dirt with my hands, mama's coming hold on baby. I love you Carla, it is dark out here in this cemetery. Out of know where these men's appeared saying, Arianna, what are you doing? my baby girl is in here and she is crying for me, please help me get her out please! One of the men said she is not there. I said yes she is"! I can hear her crying for me , the other one said she is with God in heaven remember your dream Arianna she is not here, that's just a body here. They said Jesus loves you Arianna Jesus loves you, something happened to me on the inside when I heard those words. I stop digging and looked up and the men were gone. I laid down on the grave of my daughter and cried and cried, I screamed out LORD HELP ME ! forgive me please don't leave me like this, I felt like my breath was being taking away. I can't breathe. I don't remember what happened, I don't even know how I drove home that night. The thoughts of Carla death played my mind. The next day I pick up the bible for the first time in a while and a bookmark was between the pages, I started reading and tears begin to drop from my eyes. I didn't understand why it was so important for me to forgive people, it hurted me to even think about it let alone read about forgiveness. This is what I saw in the bible.

Matthew 18:21-35 The Message (MSG)

A Story About Forgiveness

21. At that point, Peter got up the nerve to ask, "Master, how many times do I forgive a brother or sister who hurts me? Seven?"

22. Jesus replied, "Seven! Hardly. Try seventy times seven.

23-25. "The kingdom of God is like a king who decided to square accounts with his servants. As he got under way, one servant was brought before him who had run up a debt of a hundred thousand dollars. He couldn't pay up, so the king ordered the man, along with his wife, children, and goods, to be auctioned off at the slave market.

26-27. "The poor wretch threw himself at the king's feet and begged, 'Give me a chance and I'll pay it all back.' Touched by his plea, the king let him off, erasing the debt.

28. "The servant was no sooner out of the room when he came upon one of his fellow servants who owed him ten dollars. He seized him by the throat and demanded, 'Pay up. Now!'

29-31. "The poor wretch threw himself down and begged, 'Give me a chance and I'll pay it all back.' But he wouldn't do it. He had him arrested and put in jail until the debt was paid. When the other servants saw this going on, they were outraged and brought a detailed report to the king.

32-35. "The king summoned the man and said, 'You evil servant! I forgave your entire debt when you begged me for mercy. Shouldn't you be compelled to be merciful to your fellow servant who asked for mercy?' The king was furious and put the screws to the man until he paid back his entire debt. And that's exactly what my Father in heaven is going to do to each one of you who doesn't forgive unconditionally anyone who asks for mercy."

***

God spoke to me and said, Arianna, you have to forgive completely with your whole heart! I ask how can I do that? Everything in me got quiet and I heard so precise' Because I created you in my image. Because you can do all things through Christ Jesus that strengthen you, I would never put anything on you that you can't handle and Because I will always be with you. I was hearing these scriptures over and over again in my mind until I believe that I could forgive the people that had hurt me and that I had hurt with God's help, I can do it. So as God brought people in my past that had said and done hurtful things to me and people that I had hurt as well. For us to come together and talk plus apologize to each other, was unbelievable. I literally ask them to forgive me and, I felt weights lifted off my shoulders. Then I realize forgiveness was not for others but for me.

I needed God to forgive me, even though I fought with the decision to forgive myself.

***

Mourning The Death Of A Child

Absolutely nothing in life could have prepared me for the death of my child.

No matter how it happens, it was still a shock to me.It I had feelings of grief, anger, confusion, hatred, loss, bitterness, detachment, even self-blame so many emotions with the death of my child. I had to realize that I was trying to rush the grieving process. It's hard to move forward when you still in denial.

If you don't allow yourself to grieve the emotions that you are already feeling seems to get worse. One thing I learned about grief it doesn't just show up one time, grief is something that will catch you in one of those moments when you think you are doing good, when you think your pain and grief is at a point that you can handle it and, you are about to take that breath of relief, here comes grief again, it cause you to re-live one of the most painful parts of your life all over again. Now the memories of holding and loving on your child, the pain and even the fear comes back and the grieving starts all over again. I did not know want to go down that road again. Some people have said you need to only grieve for a little while. I found out that every person that lost a child their grieving process is different. Yet some people try to make it all the same, it's not.

We long to avoid this. We try to fight against grief because it terrifies us of being overwhelmed, of being misunderstood, of becoming lost in our brokenness. Because society tells us to move past this process quickly. Take days, perhaps weeks or even a few months to grieve, but don't stay there too long. I understand sometimes people don't know what to say or what to do for you when you are grieving ,it makes them feel out of place. They don't know how to handle your grief of your pain but it's not for them to handle.

For me sometimes just you begin there with me meant a lot. Family and friends try to find words to encourage you, but it doesn't always come out right. They don't understand it goes beyond words. Sometimes all you need to do is listen to the person that is grieving.

Although this heaviness of grief, is essentially painful for a period of time, it is a part of God's healing process for our life. It brings you to a place of Trusting God, and knowing that God is in Control of everything .I come to realize that you have to want to be healed. Some people just stay where they are because they don't want the memories of that child to go away so they keep holding on to the pain of it all. Afraid of letting go but tired of holding on. I truly understand that.

So every area of grief in your life gets worse instead of better because you now just existing and not living. I was there I know how it feels to have no hopes nor any dreams. Attempting to balance the emotions of grief and pain while trying to move forward with my everyday life got harder and harder for me. Until I gave myself space and time to grieve, I was honest with myself, and my emotions I had to face reality that my baby girl Carla was dead and not coming back, and I really didn't want to be healed from it . I was afraid that to be healed was to take away my memories of my child her smile, her voice, her laughter so many memories.

I came to realize that being healed was not wiping away my memories of her but it helped me to remember my daughter in an adoring way. I had to get rid of the feeling of pain an embrace Peace. I had to get rid of Who,What, When, Where, and Why. I had to somehow move passed all of those emotions and make new memories of the good ones I already had.

I begin to think about my beautiful baby girl; know matter what she went through she was always so happy she brought joy to me and many others as well. I begin to think of her beautiful eyes her smile just so beautiful, and how she could sing so beautifully those wonderful memories begin to replace those painful memories with memories of Love,Joy, Laughter, Happiness,and Peace.

I had to get to a place of wanting to be healed so I could live the life that God has for me.

I couldn't live that life holding on to unforgiveness.

So my prayer for you is that you would take out the who, what, when, where and why. And focus on the One that's in charge of everything and that is GOD. I realize that my mind, my meditation,my mouth, my momentum and my movement all had to change.

I had to change to allow God to heal me that I may live the life he has for me.

We All have endured some death in our life whether it was a Father, Mother, brother, sister, relative, a friend, even a child.

We all grieve differently.Some of us reach out to family and friends and others reach out to other things for help, But I would like to encourage you to reach out to GOD.

***

A Reflecting Moment

As the months went by one day I was I sitting in my bedroom looking over my life thus far. Many things had happened all because of the decision I had made, and because of that one decision, I felt like I had lost in life. It hurt just thinking about the pain of it all as tears roll down my cheeks, thinking about my baby girl my first born. As I begin to think about the plans that was made for her and how they will never happen. At that moment my baby girl Tyra comes in the room and gets in my lap and say I love you mother, and wrapped her little hands around me with a big hug. I held Tyra in my arms and rocked back and forth my mind traveled back even the more. I remember when my baby girl Carla was 3 1/2 years old she asks me for a baby sister. I looked at her and said a WHAT? She said a baby sister. She was for real, I said baby girl right now mommy can't do that, she said please. I said I will buy you another doll. She just looked at me with her eyes looking sad. I said what if we go to the store and get you something pretty and go get some ice cream!

She said yes mommy. I had to change that conversation with her quick.

I am in a relationship with a man that I am trying to get away from and the last thing I need by him is a child. I have been trying to leaveEric and it was not easy because Carla called him dad. I met him when Carla was 3 mos old he had made me feel so miserable. Eric was so jealous and very abusive, but his love for Carla was amazing that was the only reason why I put up with him. He was always there for her. Eric was like a dose of medicine to Carla when she was sick in the hospital or not feeling well he comes in the room and she would perk up. Other people could see it too.

When Eric came over one afternoon Carla ran to him jump in his arms daddy,daddy she said, I want a baby sister. He said a What? She said a baby sister, he said daddy can't make that promise right now you have to get better, she said please daddy he said we will see. She comes in the kitchen where I was and said mommy, daddy said he will see about me getting a baby sister. I said okay Carla go and play with your toys, I will be in there in a few minutes. Eric comes where I was and said our baby girl want a sister what do you think? Nope, I said, to my surprise, he said I agree with you A.J, What" you are agreeing with me, Eric?. He said yes I am, then he said after all this time and you're not pregnant by now maybe it's not meant to be I said you are so right. So we moved passed it. Months had passed I begin to feel sick. I finally went to my doctor thinking that my blood levels had dropped,, my blood was ok but, I was 17 weeks pregnant,feeling all kind of emotions saying this can't be happening to me. I remember calling Eric at work to ask him if we could talk when he got off work? He was very rude with me because I had broken off our engagement just some days ago ,he asked me why did I need to speak to him? Because he had other plans. I said okay whatever" I am pregnant and I hung up, I had no words on how I felt. When I got home Carla met me at the door mommy you ok, I said yes mommy is fine my baby girl, mommy just needs to rest. How could I tell her that I am going to have her a baby sister. Its like I knew it was a girl maybe because Carla had been asking and say it for so long and now it's true. So much was going on in my mind about this baby like it has to be a reason for her, After all this time why now! I didn't know why I kept saying her. Carla got sick and had to be admitted into the hospital again. I told her that she was going to be a big sister soon. I had to give her something to hope for. Her little face lit up with so much joy.

When I had Tyra, Carla was a proud big sister, She wanted to hold her little sister every chance she could. Oh, wow so much love they had for each other.

As I look back on all of this tears streamed down my face even more. I held Tyra closer to me rocking her until she fell asleep. I laid her down. Thinking that Carla didn't want me to be alone. Tyra was the only hope I had and I cling to her for life to live. Even thinking about the home going services I could not make the arrangements because I was telling myself she was not dead. I thought that for awhile my sisters did arrangements for the home going service for Carla I still feel so weak like I am just existing but not living .I have cried an ocean of tears.

As am wiping my face I heard a voice that said read Corinthians 12:9 I replied forreal 'No more Bible. I tried that look where I am, look at my LIFE, I am in a relationship with a man that abused me and I have a baby by him and I don't know how to get out of it. My family is in there own little world and A.J. is nowhere in it. I feel like I am an outcast. I am the black sheep of my family, I really think that I'm no sheep in this family No one new how I really felt . On top of all of that, my daughter is dead! " And you want me to read some scriptures. Nope, I don't think so, And I went out of my room Tyra was taking a nap. I went into the living room my mom was talking to her best friend Evangelist Wright seem like they were just getting started my mom took Carla death very hard, but she had her family and church family, job and her best friend But most of all she had God.

When they started talking hours pass by my mom said Evangelist this scripture has been in my spirit, 2 Corinthians 12:9 I could hear Evangelist Wright say AMEN".

I was like for real I don't have to listen to that. I left out and went back into my room. My mom was reading so loud normally she's whispering.

Ok ok ok ! I guess I'll read it. I got the bible and read.

2 CORINTHIANS 12:9 But he said to me my grace is sufficient for you , for my powers is made perfect in weakness ."Therefore ,I will boast all the more gladly about my weakness so that Christ's power may rest on me. That is why , for Christ sake , I delight in weakness, in insults, in hardships, in persecutions , in difficulties , for when I am weak, then I am strong.

Okay, I read it now what? reading that does not bring my daughter back.

What I have come to realize is that I did not want help from God, I was hurting and I wanted to stay there why should I live on in this world and laughter and move forward without my daughter just let me be.

Just as quick as I had spoken it , my life had made a turn to the unknown the sounds I heard negative words that said it's all your fault AJ Just kill yourself

,so many screaming sounds, words coming all-from this place of the unknown I tried to block out the noise, sounds, and words but I couldn't, all of sudden I felt like I was carrying bricks in and on me I was so heavy . I needed help as days,weeks and even months went by every day, I existed only for my daughter Tyra but I was getting weaker in my mind and body. I started seeing things and people that were not of this world. I felt like I was about to go insane, I felt empty but yet heavy and confused, I felt so alone, I felt like my strength was leavening me I felt no peace or reassurance my mind playing tricks on me. I could not sleep I tossed and turned,I took pills, I can't do this.I need God and I needed him now. As I cried out LORD HELP ME!!!!! , something happen all the voices stop. That was in my head, everything became bright like, I had been in a dark room and someone opens the blinds and the sun came in and lite up every area of darkness. I didn't feel like I was carrying heavy weights any longer. I felt lighter, stronger, my mind was clear, I could focus.I can hear songs and beautiful singing it had to be angels from heaven, God had them to sing over me. At that moment I felt like Jesus had come and poured so much love on me. My mind had changed about people, and even myself. It's like I see things differently now. I can't describe how I felt I had no words for it, all I know is that I wish I could have stayed in that place forever. It was like everything that had happened, was for a reason and it was ok. I felt like I had so many people around me saying how much they love me and saying forgive AJ forgive. My mind race with-who are those people, and how can they love me? I will forgive, I will forgive. I am answering them like they were right in the car with me, but I was so excited about where I was it was a blissful place, and I wanted to stay there forever, I heard a voice say you have to Forgive.

***

MY PERSONAL THOUGHTS ABOUT E.G.P

"The Emotions of Grief, and Pain, of losing a child, I had to realize that there are no E.G.P management programs that can help me during this process, Grief is a lot of mixed emotions that goes deeper and deeper each and every time, If I don't allow the process to take its course.

To me, grief was like a brook, a stream, a river, a lake, the sea even the ocean you can see it touch it taste it hear it and even smell it but we can not control it. It's like our emotions, grief, and pain. You can't control it you have to allow yourself to go through the process. This let me know that I was not in control that I need God to help me yet, I knew that it did not stop my heart from hurting of pain and grief, so my emotions became untameable like an ocean in a storm. In the middle of my storm, I realized that I was about to drown in the ocean of my tears. I had to scream out God Help Me"! God pulled me out of my own ocean of tears, emotions, grief, and pain. It was not that I did not have these emotions or grief, and even pain But something happen within my mind. My mind started to change how I looked at my emotions, grief, and pain.

As I read these scriptures below something happen to me.My Mind was changing. Yes I still cried ,yes I still felt the pain and yes I grieved, But something happen,I realize that I had no HOPE , but when I grab a hold of HOPE something great happen to me.

Here are a few scriptures I would like to share with you. We can turn to God's word for Comfort, Encouragement,Healing,   Peace,   Love,Forgiveness and Hope Be healed and live the life God has for you.

These scriptures are taken from the New International Version Bible.

1 Thessalonians 4:13 Brothers and Sister, we do not want you to be uninformed about those who sleep in death so that you do not grieve like the rest of mankind,who have no HOPE.

Revelation 21:4 'He will wipe every tear from their eyes. There will be no more death' or mourning or crying or pain, for the old order of things has passed away."

Psalm 34:18 The LORD is close to the brokenhearted and saves those who are crushed in spirit.

Psalm 147:3 He heals the brokenhearted and binds up their wounds.

Deuteronomy 31:8 The Lord himself goes before you and will be with you ;he will never leave you nor forsake you. Don't be afraid; do not be discouraged."

Psalm 30:2 O Lord my God ,I cried unto thee,and thou hast healed me .

Joshua 1:9 Have I not commanded you? Be strong and courageous. Do not be afraid; do not be discouraged, for the LORD your God will be with you wherever you go."

Matthew 5:4 Blessed are those who mourn, for they will be comforted.

Isaiah 41:10 So don't fear, for I am with you; do not be dismayed , for I am your God . I will strengthen you and help you; I will uphold you with my righteous right hand.

John 14:1-3 "Do not let your hearts be troubled. You believe in God [a]; believe also in me.

My Father's house has many rooms; if that were not so, would I have told you that I am going there to prepare a place for you? And if I go and prepare a place for you, I will come back and take you to be with me that you also may be where I am.

John 11:25-26 "Jesus said to her, 'I am the resurrection and the life. The one who believes in me will live, even though they die; and whoever lives by believing in me will never die. Do you believe this?'"

2 Corinthians 4:17-18 "For our light and momentary troubles are achieving for us an eternal glory that far outweighs them all. So we fix our eyes not on what is seen, but on what is unseen, since what is seen is temporary, but what is unseen is eternal."

Isaiah 41:10 "So do not fear, for I am with you; do not be dismayed, for I am your God. I will strengthen you and help you. I will uphold you with my righteous right hand."

***

Prayer

Father God in the name of Jesus, I pray for every person and families that is going through the death of a child. Father wrap your healing ,loving arms around them, comfort them and give the strength and peace only like you can. Father if they are having any emotions of guilt, self blame, anger, unforgiveness, regret, bitterness, depression, even fear, Father I thank you for removing those emotions and replace them with your, love, patience, peace, forgiveness, joy, and laughter, as they remember the happy moments about their child.

In Jesus Name Amen

***

I came to realize that there is no cure for grief neither is there a fast fix but you have to be willing to go through the process to heal so that you can live your best life, that God has planned for you. I pray that these words Encourage, Comfort, and Strengthen you

.

- I will pray

- I will meditate (Listen to God)

- I am walking in my healing now.

- I allowed myself to feel again.

- I will not lay in grief.

- I will let go and grab hold to God .

- I'm walking through grief.

- I'm walking by faith not by sight.

- Only God can heal the void in my heart.

- My loved one doesn't live in my grief, and pain they live in my Heart.

- I am getting better every day.

- I feel strength, love, peace and comfort around me every day.

- I'm not going to hold back my tears they will flow in freedom.

- Every morning is beautiful to me.

- I have great memories of my baby.

- I will accept help when it's extended.

- I will ask for help when I need it.

- I am not alone.

- I'm grateful for the time we had together.

- I am patient with myself as I heal.

- I forgive myself.

- I forgive others.

- I am thinking positive thoughts.

- I think about how my loved one lived not how they died.

- I will not be afraid to live the life God has for me.